Jackie Jack

THE BRAVE LITTLE BOY

Jackie Jack

THE BRAVE LITTLE BOY

Julie Orlet-Schoen

Illustrations by
Renee Orlet Comerford

WOODLAND STUDIOS, INC.

Belleville, Illinois • 1998

WOODLAND STUDIOS·INC

Copyright © 1998 by Julie Orlet-Schoen

ISBN 0-9663076-0-7 hard cover
ISBN 0-9663076-1-5 soft cover

Library of Congress Catalog Card Number: 98-060576

Typography and production assistance by Village Typographers, Inc.

Printed in the United States of America

Woodland Studios, Inc.
P. O. Box 364
Belleville, IL 62222-0364
618-236-1881

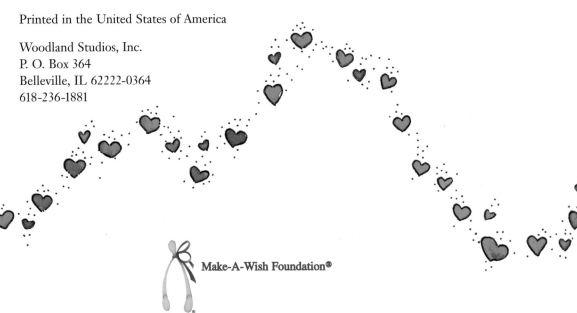

Make-A-Wish Foundation®

*Five percent of the royalties from the sale of this book
will benefit the Make-A-Wish Foundation.*

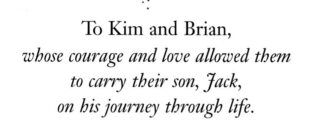

To Kim and Brian,
whose courage and love allowed them
to carry their son, Jack,
on his journey through life.

Jackie Jack came into this world
like all blessed children . . .
into the arms of a Mama and Papa
who loved him very, very much.

He had eyes blue like the ocean,
hair brown like the earth,
and a smile as big as all outdoors.

Jackie Jack felt the warmth of
the sun, the coolness of the breeze,
and the gentleness of the rain
as he learned of his world.

Jackie Jack would wrap his tiny
arms around his Mama and Papa
and he would smile his smile,
which was as big as all outdoors.

Mama and Papa would smile
back at their baby boy,
who brought them such joy.

One day, Jackie Jack became very, very sick and had to go to the hospital. He was afraid, but Mama and Papa were brave, and their love for him helped Jackie Jack be brave.

At night in the hospital,
Mama would climb into bed
next to her baby boy and wrap
her strong arms around him.

Jackie Jack would sleep,
dreaming of the warmth of the sun,
the coolness of the breeze,
the gentleness of the rain . . .
and his Mama's love . . .
and he felt very peaceful indeed.

During the day, Papa would hold
his son on his knee and wrap
his great big arms around him.

Jackie Jack would rest,
dreaming of the warmth of the sun,
the coolness of the breeze,
the gentleness of the rain . . .
and his Papa's love . . .
and he felt very peaceful indeed.

Jackie Jack would smile his smile,
which was as big as all outdoors,
at Mama and Papa, Tom the Janitor,
Mr. Snackman, and all the doctors
and nurses who came to visit
him in his room. They looked into
his eyes, which were blue like the ocean,
and they felt his love . . . and his love
helped them be strong.

One night, the doctors and the nurses, Tom the Janitor, and Mr. Snackman said goodbye to Jackie Jack.

Then, Jackie Jack went home.

Jackie Jack was very, very tired.
He slept between Mama and Papa
in their big bed.

During the night Jackie Jack
woke up. He saw a beautiful light
above his head and heard the
lovely voices of a thousand angels.

He reached for the beautiful light
and the lovely angels, but being very,
very tired, he could not touch them.

Mama and Papa, whose love
for Jackie Jack made him very strong,
whispered, "Jackie Jack, our brave
little boy, go to the light . . . jump
to the angels . . . and don't look back."

And Jackie Jack listened.

He jumped as high as he could,
toward the beautiful light and
the lovely voices of a thousand angels.

And then . . . he rested . . .
in the arms of a thousand angels,
who loved him very, very much.

Mama and Papa rested
in each other's arms,
dreaming of the warmth of the sun,
the coolness of the breeze,
the gentleness of the rain . . .
and their baby's love.

When they awoke, having become very strong and brave from their Jackie Jack's love, Mama and Papa climbed a very tall mountain.

At the top, they felt the tiny arms
of their Jackie Jack wrapped
around them, and they felt his love
in the warmth of the sun,
in the coolness of the breeze,
and in the gentleness of the rain.

They looked up to the heavens
and they saw his smile, which was
as big as all outdoors, and they knew
their Jackie Jack was free.

They heard the sound of
the wind and the lovely voices
of a thousand . . . and one . . . angels,
and they felt very peaceful indeed.

THE BEGINNING

After John "Jack" Graeme Edwards was diagnosed with leukemia, his parents, Kim and Brian, spent the remainder of his life searching for a cure for their son.

Jack spent much of his life in Primary Children's Hospital in Salt Lake City, Utah. His parents took turns sleeping next to him in his hospital crib.

Near the end, Kim and Brian decided to take their son home to their own bed. Moments before Jack died, he pointed toward a beautiful light that only he could see and asked, "What's that?" By their encouragement, Kim and Brian allowed their baby to follow the light and finally experience the peace he deserved. Jack was 21 months old.

After a memorial service, Kim and Brian carried their baby's ashes to the top of a mountain. Together they released their Jackie Jack to the wind and returned him to Mother Nature.

ABOUT THE AUTHOR

Days after Jack died, Julie wrote *Jackie Jack—The Brave Little Boy* as a gift to Kim and Brian Edwards.

Kim's response to the book was, "It sounds like my little angel inspired you. Thank you for listening." With encouragement from Kim and Brian, Julie decided to share Jack's story.

Julie is a freelance writer. She lives in Belleville, Illinois with her husband, Joe, and their four children.

ABOUT THE ARTIST

As a friend of Kim and Brian Edwards, Renee had spent time with Jack during his illness.

Her creation of these beautiful watercolors proved to be an aid in her own healing process and provides a vivid affirmation of Jack's brief life.

Renee is a professional artist. She lives in Springfield, Illinois with her husband, Steve, and their two children.